THE CASE OF THE
Singing Ocean

Eric Hogan & Tara Hungerford

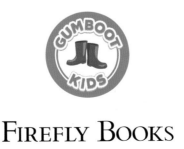

GUMBOOT KIDS

FIREFLY BOOKS

**For Wilfred, Paris and Gumboot Kids
all around the world.**

Published Under License by Firefly Books Ltd. 2020
Copyright © 2020 Gumboot Kids Media Inc.
Book adaptation and realization © 2020 Firefly Books Ltd.
Photographs © Gumboot Kids Media Inc. unless otherwise
specified on page 32.

This book is based on the popular children's shows *Scout &
the Gumboot Kids*, *Daisy & the Gumboot Kids* and *Jessie &
the Gumboot Kids*.

First printing

Library of Congress Control Number: 2020936491

Library and Archives Canada Cataloguing in Publication:
Title: The case of the singing ocean / Eric Hogan & Tara Hungerford.
Other titles: Singing ocean | Scout & the Gumboot Kids (Television
program)
Names: Hogan, Eric, 1979- author. | Hungerford, Tara, 1975- author.
Series: Hogan, Eric, 1979- Gumboot Kids nature mystery.
Description: Series statement: A Gumboot Kids nature mystery
Identifiers: Canadiana 20200226185 | ISBN 9780228102854 (hard-
cover) | ISBN 9780228102847 (softcover)
Subjects: LCSH: Whale sounds—Juvenile literature. | LCSH:
Whales—Juvenile literature.
Classification: LCC QL737.C4 H64 2020 | DDC j599.5—dc23

Published in the United States by
Firefly Books (U.S.) Inc.
P.O. Box 1338, Ellicott Station
Buffalo, New York 14205

Published in Canada by
Firefly Books Ltd.
50 Staples Avenue, Unit 1
Richmond Hill, Ontario L4B 0A7

Printed in China

Canada ▮▮ We acknowledge the financial support
of the Government of Canada.

Scout and Daisy are out for a nature walk. Today they're at the ocean, walking along the beach.

"Isn't the ocean mesmerizing?" says Daisy as she takes a deep breath. "Ahhhh! And I love the smell of the salty sea air."

"I do, too," says Scout. "And I love the soothing sound of the waves."

Scout and Daisy close their eyes and listen to the ocean.

A trio of seagulls swoop overhead. *KEOW! KEOW! KEOW!*

"Well, it just got a lot noisier here. We may not be able to hear the ocean singing," says Scout.

"Wait—what? You've heard the ocean singing?" asks Daisy.

"Yes, I heard the ocean singing this morning," says Scout. "It was the most mysterious sound I've ever heard!"

"Well, this sounds like a nature mystery," says Daisy. "The Case of the Singing Ocean!"

Scout cracks open his field notes.

"Check it out. I made some sketches on my morning walk," says Scout. "Maybe they'll help us solve the mystery."

"It's a cliff!" says Daisy. "That path over there leads to the cliff. Let's go!"

Cliff

Scout and Daisy wind their way up the path to reach a lookout at the top of the cliff.

They pause, look around and listen.

"I can sure see a lot from up here," observes Daisy, "but I don't hear any singing."

"What else did you notice on your morning walk?" asks Daisy.

Scout opens his field notes.

"That's a tail!" remarks Daisy.

Tail

Daisy peers through her binoculars and scans the ocean. "I see something swimming in the ocean ... and it has a tail! Check it out."

Daisy passes the binoculars to Scout.

"Wow!" exclaims Scout. "That looks just like the tail I saw this morning."

While Scout looks through the binoculars, Daisy flips to the next clue in the field notes. "You drew a splash," says Daisy. "I wonder what caused that?"

Suddenly, a huge creature lifts itself out of the ocean and lands back in the water with a big *SPLASH*.

"It's a whale!" exclaims Scout. "A humpback whale!"

"Wow!" Scout and Daisy say together as they look on in wonder.

Splash

A moment later the whale is nowhere to be seen, but Daisy hears something. "Do you hear that low whistling sound, Scout?"

"I do," replies Scout. "How curious."

"I know where we can find out more," says Daisy, excitedly. "To the library!"

At her library, Daisy grabs a book about whales. She flips it open and eagerly scans the pages. "Aha!" she says, "I found it!"

She shares the book with Scout, who reads aloud:

"Whales are marine mammals that are able to make loud, melodic notes and tones. Marine biologists call these sounds 'whale songs.' A whale song can travel far through the ocean as sound waves, so it can sound like the ocean is singing. Marine biologists have observed whales singing different songs to communicate different things."

"So it was whales singing in the ocean!" says Scout.

"We did it!" says Daisy. "We solved The Case of the Singing Ocean!"

Later that evening, Scout and Daisy raise their hot chocolate in celebration.

"Hooray!"

"Now let's pause and have a mindful moment," says Scout. "One of the ways in which animals communicate is with sound. Many animals, like birds and whales, make noises that sound like music."

Daisy continues, "The next time you're outside in nature, close your eyes and pay attention to the sounds around you. What sounds are close to you? What sounds are far away? Do you hear birds singing or insects buzzing? What other sounds do you notice?"

The next day Scout and Daisy walk back to the lookout by the ocean. Scout has brought his oboe and Daisy her violin. They play a jaunty song.

"Do you hear that?" asks Daisy. "The ocean is singing with us!"

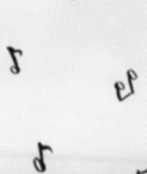

Field Notes

Rostrum: The rostrum is another word for a whale's upper jaw or snout.

Blowholes: Whales breathe through their blowholes like nostrils.

Flukes: The flukes are the two lobes of a whale's tail. The flukes move up and down propelling the animal through the water.

Fins: The fins are used for steering underwater.

Ears: Sound is the dominant sense for whales. They use sound to navigate, communicate and find food.

Humpback Whale

Flukes

Blowholes

Rostrum

Fin

Ear

Whales are a highly intelligent species and deep thinkers. In fact, they are known to have remarkable abilities, including adapting to change, recognizing, remembering, reasoning, communicating and problem-solving.

Whales are mammals because they give live birth and provide milk for their young. They also have hair and lungs and they breathe air.

Whales live in every ocean and they are the largest animals on Earth. The blue whale is the longest whale (29.9 meters/98.1 feet) — almost as long as a basketball court!

There are two types of whales, toothed whales and baleen whales. Toothed whales have teeth and they actively hunt fish and other sea creatures. Baleen whales have bristly baleen plates attached to their upper jaws. To feed, they take huge gulps of seawater and then push the water back out through the plates. This is how they strain and catch prey like krill and tiny shrimp.

Toothed whales include dolphins, sperm whales, porpoises and orcas.

Baleen whales include humpback, fin, blue and gray whales.

Nature Craft

Daisy was so inspired by her time with Scout at the beach that she made some sand art. Would you like to make some sand art, too?

STEP 1

The next time you're at the beach, collect some sand and shells or other small treasures. Only take what there's lots of and only take a little bit.

STEP 2

Gather paper, glitter, glue and watercolor paints or felt-tip pens. Draw an outline of something that you saw at the beach. Maybe a sea star, a fish or some waves.

STEP 3

Outline or fill in your shape with glue. While the glue is still wet, sprinkle glitter, sand, shells and other treasures on top. Carefully shake off any excess sand and let your paper dry. Voila!

TELEVISION SERIES CREDITS

Created by Eric Hogan and Tara Hungerford
Produced by Tracey Mack
Developed for television with Cathy Moss
Music by Jessie Farrell

Education Consultants
Mindfulness: Molly Stewart Lawlor, Ph.D
Zoology: Michelle Tseng, Ph.D
Botany: Loren Rieseberg, Ph.D

BOOK CREDITS

Based on scripts for television by Eric Hogan,
Tara Hungerford and Cathy Moss
Production Design: Eric Hogan and Tara Hungerford
Head of Production: Tracey Mack
Character Animation: Jon Affolter
Photography: Thomas Affolter
Graphic Design: Rio Trenaman
Illustration: Kate Jeong

Special thanks to the Gumboot Kids cast and crew,
CBC Kids, Shaw Rocket Fund, Independent Media
Fund, The Bell Fund, Canada Media Fund, Creative
BC and our friends and family.

ADDITIONAL PHOTO CREDITS

Shutterstock.com: 17 CHANUN.V; 19 davidhoffmann
photography; 22-23 (whales) Imagine Earth
Photography, (tabletop) primopiano; 24 (fire) fire art,
(steam) George Dolgikh; 29 (top left) Andrea Izzotti,
(top right) Christopher Meder, (middle) Andrew Sutton,
(bottom left) Christian Musat, (bottom right) jo Crebbin;
30 (sand) Big Foot Productions, (paint) Vadym Zaitsev,
(glue) Mega Pixel

More GUMBOOT KIDS Nature Mysteries

For Gumboot Kids episodes, music and curriculum guides, visit GUMBOOTKIDS.COM

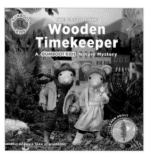